PERCY JACKSON & THE OLYMPIANS

BOOK THREE

THE TITAN'S CURSE
The Graphic Novel

by
RICK RIORDAN

Adapted by
Robert Venditti

Art by
Attila Futaki

Color by
Gregory Guilhaumond

Lettering by
Chris Dickey

DISNEY · HYPERION BOOKS
New York

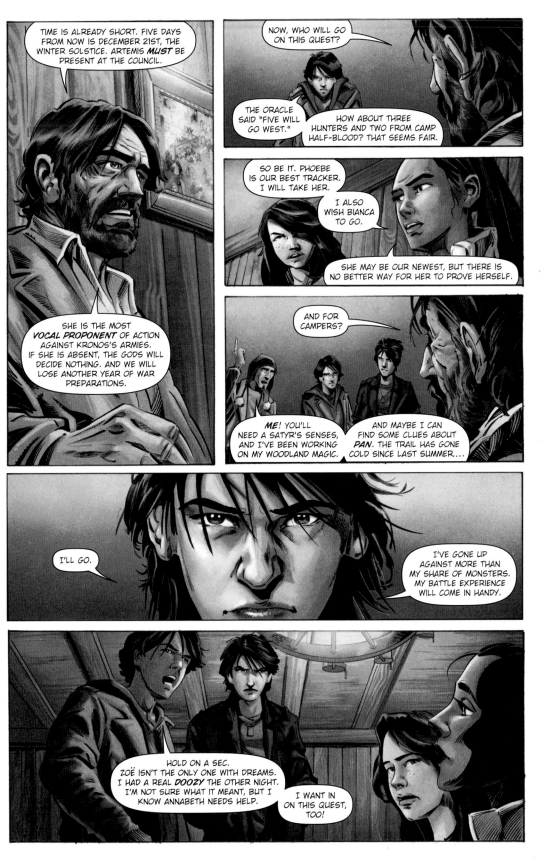

HERE YOU GO, BOSS. STRAIGHT DOWN ABOUT ONE HUNDRED FEET.

PERFECT. SHOULD BE NICE AND *WARM* DOWN THERE.

YES.
I KNOW
WHERE THE
ROOM IS.

NATIONAL MUSEUM OF
NATURAL HISTORY.

NO ADMITTANCE

DINOSAUR TEETH. HA! THOSE FOOLISH CURATORS DON'T EVEN KNOW THEY HAVE *DRAGON TEETH* IN THEIR COLLECTION.

AND NOT JUST ANY TEETH. THEY COME FROM THE ANCIENT *SYBARIS* HERSELF!

SOON, LUKE, WE WILL COMMAND SOLDIERS THAT WILL MAKE THAT ARMY ON YOUR LITTLE BOAT LOOK INSIGNIFICANT.

THEY WILL DO NICELY INDEED.

RISE! IT IS TIME TO REPORT FOR DUTY.

PERCY!

STOP HIM!

RIIIP

SNIFF
SNIFF

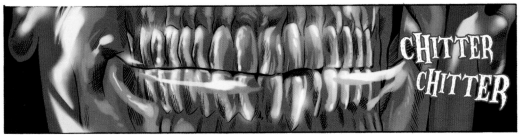

CHITTER
CHITTER

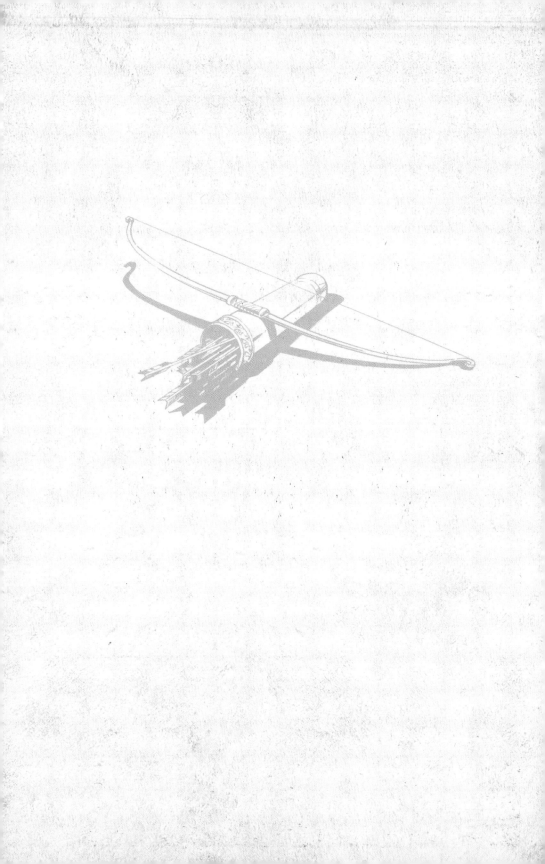

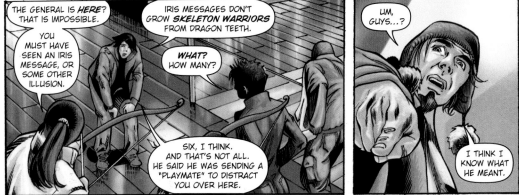

"--AND WE ARE NOT LEAVING ANYONE BEHIND."

›snort‹
›zzzzz‹

YOU SHOULD BE SLEEPING LIKE THE OTHERS.

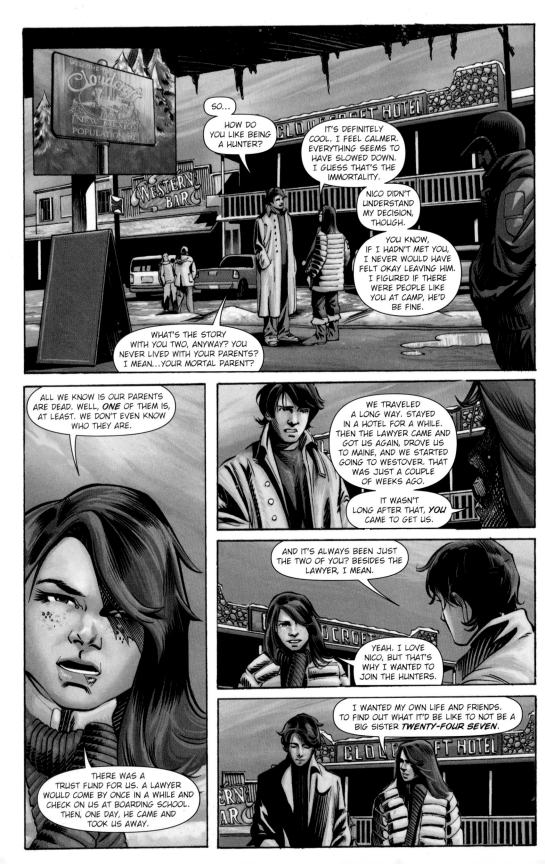

REEEEET!

FWUMP

-snrrt-

RUN!

SOMEWHERE IN ARIZONA.

THIS IS AS FAR AS THE BOAR WILL TAKE US. WE SHOULD GET OFF WHILE IT'S DRINKING.

~slurp~
~slurp~

THANKS FOR THE LIFT, PORKY!

WHERE ARE WE?

WHEREVER WE ARE, I *HIGHLY DOUBT* WE'LL BE ABLE TO FIND A RENTAL CAR.

GUYS? WHAT ARE *THOSE?*

WE ARE ON THE EDGE OF ONE OF *HEPHAESTUS'S JUNKYARDS*. IT IS WHERE HE DISCARDS ALL HIS FAILED MACHINES AND INVENTIONS.

AND THE PATH TO ARTEMIS LEADS STRAIGHT THROUGH IT.

I DO NOT LIKE THIS. LET US REST UNTIL NIGHTFALL. WE WILL CROSS THE JUNKYARD AT NIGHT WHEN IT IS COOLER.

AND WHEN WE WILL BE LESS EASY TO DETECT.

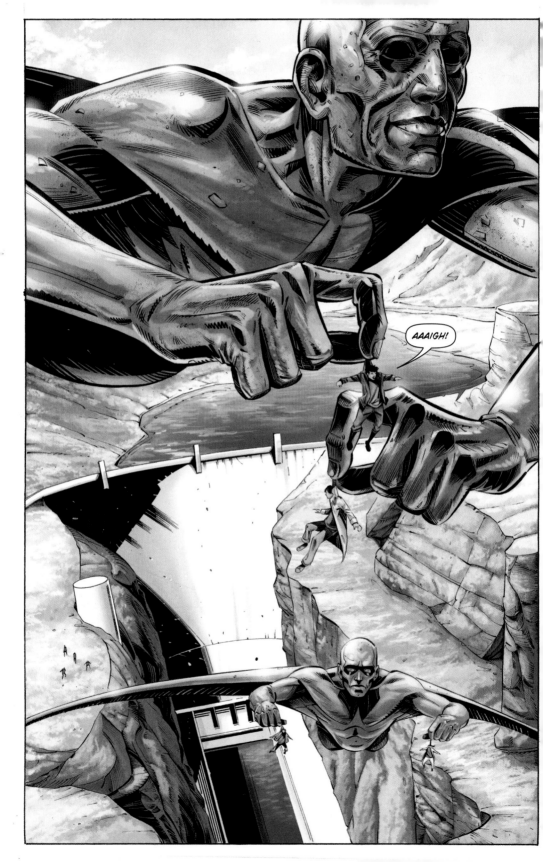

YAH!

Z-ZZT

YOU'LL HAVE TO DO BETTER THAN THAT!

SKRRCH

FOOLISH BOY.

ANCIENT LAWS FORBID AN IMMORTAL FROM DIRECTLY CHALLENGING A HERO.

CLACK

BUT NOW THAT *YOU* HAVE CHALLENGED *ME*--

-:nng:-

WHAM

--I AM FREE TO CHALLENGE IN KIND.

-:unff:-

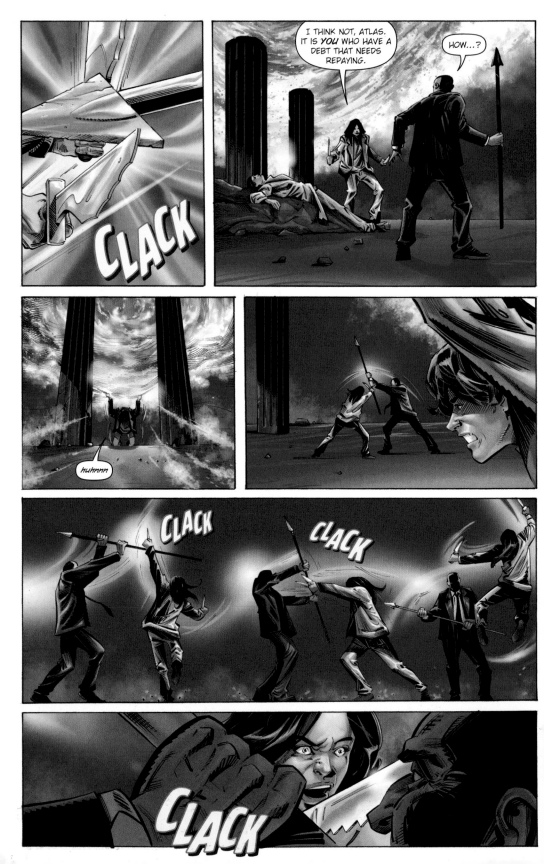

SMACK

FINALLY. THE FIRST BLOOD OF A *NEW WAR.*

NO!

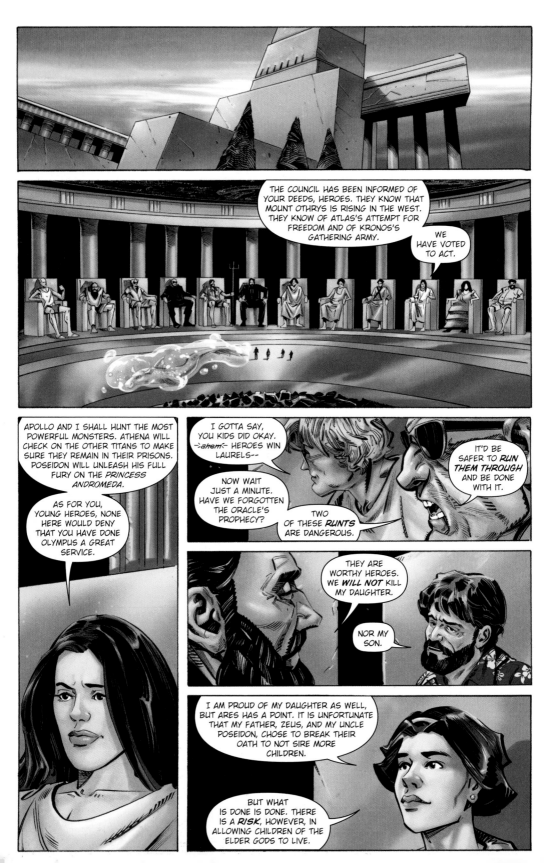

THE COUNCIL HAS BEEN INFORMED OF YOUR DEEDS, HEROES. THEY KNOW THAT MOUNT OTHRYS IS RISING IN THE WEST. THEY KNOW OF ATLAS'S ATTEMPT FOR FREEDOM AND OF KRONOS'S GATHERING ARMY.

WE HAVE VOTED TO ACT.

APOLLO AND I SHALL HUNT THE MOST POWERFUL MONSTERS. ATHENA WILL CHECK ON THE OTHER TITANS TO MAKE SURE THEY REMAIN IN THEIR PRISONS. POSEIDON WILL UNLEASH HIS FULL FURY ON THE *PRINCESS ANDROMEDA*.

AS FOR YOU, YOUNG HEROES, NONE HERE WOULD DENY THAT YOU HAVE DONE OLYMPUS A GREAT SERVICE.

I GOTTA SAY, YOU KIDS DID OKAY. –*ahem*– HEROES WIN LAURELS--

IT'D BE SAFER TO *RUN THEM THROUGH* AND BE DONE WITH IT.

NOW WAIT JUST A MINUTE. HAVE WE FORGOTTEN THE ORACLE'S PROPHECY?

TWO OF THESE *RUNTS* ARE DANGEROUS.

THEY ARE WORTHY HEROES. WE *WILL NOT* KILL MY DAUGHTER.

NOR MY SON.

I AM PROUD OF MY DAUGHTER AS WELL, BUT ARES HAS A POINT. IT IS UNFORTUNATE THAT MY FATHER, ZEUS, AND MY UNCLE POSEIDON, CHOSE TO BREAK THEIR OATH TO NOT SIRE MORE CHILDREN.

BUT WHAT IS DONE IS DONE. THERE IS A *RISK*, HOWEVER, IN ALLOWING CHILDREN OF THE ELDER GODS TO LIVE.

"LET THE TRIUMPH CELEBRATION BEGIN."

YOU, UH, OKAY THERE, G-MAN?

S-SURE.

I'M JUST GOING TO KEEP D-DRINKING THESE TRIPLE ESPRESSO LATTES UNTIL I GET ANOTHER SIGN F-FROM PAN....

YOU WON'T LET ME DOWN, I HOPE.

I'LL J-JUST BE G-G-GOING.

THANKS FOR STICKING UP FOR ME, DAD. I WON'T LET YOU DOWN. I PROMISE.

LUKE ONCE PROMISED HIS FATHER THAT. HE WAS HERMES'S PRIDE AND JOY. JUST BEAR THAT IN MIND, PERCY. EVEN THE BRAVEST CAN FALL.

LUKE FELL *PRETTY HARD*, ALL RIGHT. RIGHT OFF THE TOP OF MOUNT OTHRYS. HE'S DEAD.

NO, HE IS NOT.

LUKE SAILS WITH HIS SHIP FROM SAN FRANCISCO EVEN NOW. HE WILL RETREAT AND REGROUP BEFORE ASSAULTING YOU AGAIN.

I DON'T KNOW HOW HE SURVIVED, BUT HE IS MORE DANGEROUS THAN EVER. AND THE GOLDEN COFFIN IS STILL WITH HIM, *KRONOS* STILL GAINING STRENGTH.

YOU DID WELL, MY SON, BUT YOUR ROLE IN THIS IS NOT YET RESOLVED. PREPARE YOURSELF. CONTINUE YOUR TRAINING, AND I KNOW YOU WILL MAKE ME PROUD.

YOUR FATHER TAKES A GREAT RISK, YOU KNOW. WISE COUNSEL IS NOT ALWAYS POPULAR, BUT I SPOKE THE TRUTH.

YOU *ARE* DANGEROUS.

FIRST, YOUR MOTHER WAS TAKEN FROM YOU. THEN, YOUR BEST FRIEND, GROVER.

NOW MY DAUGHTER. IN EACH CASE, YOUR LOVED ONES HAVE BEEN USED TO LURE YOU INTO KRONOS'S TRAPS.

THE CROOKED ONE KNOWS HOW TO STUDY HIS ENEMIES. HE KNOWS YOUR *FATAL FLAW*, EVEN IF YOU DO NOT. AND HE WILL CONTINUE TO USE IT AGAINST YOU.

YOUR FATAL FLAW IS *PERSONAL LOYALTY*.

TO SAVE A FRIEND, YOU WOULD SACRIFICE THE WORLD. IN A HERO OF THE PROPHECY, THAT IS A VERY DANGEROUS THING.

IF HELPING THE PEOPLE YOU CARE ABOUT IS A FLAW, THEN YOU'RE GUILTY OF IT, TOO.

AFTER ALL, *YOU* WERE THE PARK RANGER AT THE HOOVER DAM, RIGHT?

THEN DON'T WORRY ABOUT ME, MOM. I LIKE HIM BETTER THAN GABE ALREADY.

I'LL SEE YOU FOR CHRISTMAS?

ABSOLUTELY! THERE WILL BE *EXTRA CANDY* IN YOUR STOCKING THIS YEAR, TOO.

I'LL MAKE SURE OF IT.

AND PERCY? THANK YOU.

OKAY, MOM. SEE YOU SOON.

KNOCK KNOCK

HEY! ~huff huff~ I HEARD YOU WERE BACK. WHERE'S BIANCA? I WANT TO HEAR ALL ABOUT HER *ADVENTURE!*

NICO, WE NEED TO TALK....

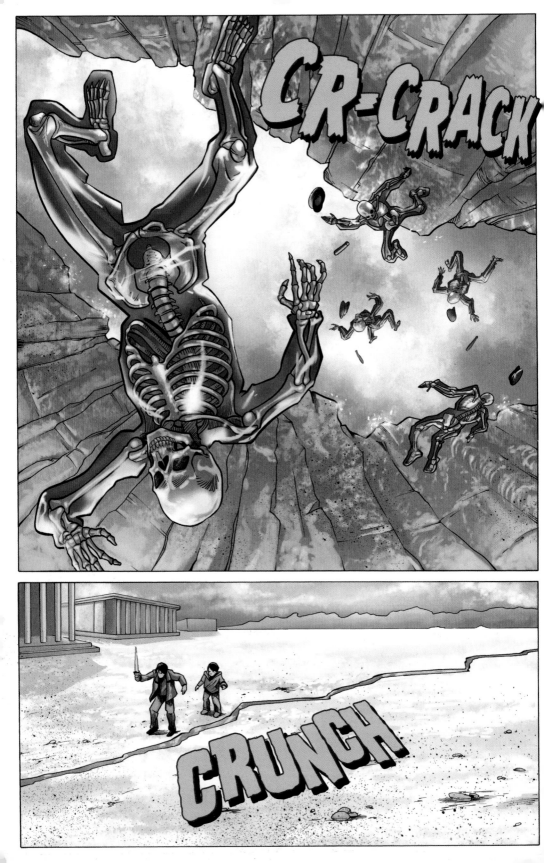

HE SPOKE! HE SPOKE!

GROVER?! **NOW** WHAT'S WRONG?

I WAS DRINKING COFFEE. LOTS OF COFFEE. AND **PAN** SPOKE IN MY MIND. THE LORD OF THE WILD HIMSELF.

HE SAID--

--"*I AWAIT YOU.*"

END OF BOOK 3.

Adapted from the novel
Percy Jackson & the Olympians, Book Three: *The Titan's Curse*

Text copyright © 2013 by Rick Riordan
Illustrations copyright © 2013 Disney Enterprises, Inc.

Design by Jim Titus

Printed in the United States of America
V381-8386-5-13196
First Edition
10 9 8 7 6 5 4 3 2 1

Library of Congress Cataloging-in-Publication Data
The Titan's curse : the graphic novel / by Rick Riordan ; adapted by Robert Venditti ;
art by Attila Futaki ; lettering by Chris Dickey.—1st ed.
    p. cm.— (Percy Jackson & the Olympians ; bk. 3)
    "Adapted from the novel Percy Jackson & the Olympians, Book Three: The Titan's Curse"—T.p. verso.
    Summary: When the goddess Artemis disappears while hunting a rare, ancient monster, a group of her
followers joins Percy and his friends in an attempt to find and rescue her before the winter solstice, when
her influence is needed to sway the Olympian Council regarding the war with the Titans.
    ISBN 978-1-4231-4530-1 (hardcover)—ISBN 978-1-4231-4551-6 (paperback)
    1. Graphic novels. [1. Graphic novels. 2. Mythology, Greek—Fiction. 3. Artemis (Greek deity)—Fiction
4. Animals, Mythical—Fiction. 5. Monsters—Fiction. 6. Titans (Mythology)—Fiction. 7. Riordan, Rick.
Titan's curse—Adaptations.] I. Futaki, Attila, ill. II. Riordan, Rick. Titan's curse. III. Title.
PZ7.7.V48Ti 2013
741.5'973—dc23   2012007895

Visit www.PercyJacksonBooks.com
and www.disneyhyperionbooks.com